Workplace Confidential

PHOENIX ON THE MAINLINE

BY: RO.ELLE

Ro.Elle Cochrane, Workplace Confidential: Phoenix on the Mainline Edited by: Jerra Mitchell Published by: SoWritePublishing, LLC

ISBN: 978-0-578-84067-3

Printed in the United States of America

This publication is designed to provide perspective information with regards to the subject matter covered. The stories described in this book are derived from truth related experiences, however the majority of the names are pseudonyms, and the scenarios have been altered to ensure complete privacy. It is sold with the understanding that the publisher is not engaged in rendering legal or professional advice. It is highly recommended that professional and legal assistance be consulted should one need it.

The author and publisher disclaim all responsibility for loss, risk, liability, personal or otherwise which could result as a consequence of directly or indirectly applying of any of the book's contents.

Dedication Page

To my mother, a woman of many talents, and my father, a man of many minds. I am because you are.

CONTENTS

No Work No Play

N o work and no play can really suck the life out of
a lady. I have been in que for the past six months,
and let's just say that your girl is overdue for some
action. I've been really feigning for a thrill, an
adventure. I need some excitement among other things,
and that list is getting longer by the day. If you were
thinking of something else, something more X-rated,
then slowly collect your thoughts from the gutter
because I'm talking about work. My last mission was
short-lived and needed to be for particularly good
reasons, but since that time, I've been waiting for the
next one. Marshall Eagle or "M.E.", my boss in
headquarters continues to reassign my missions to the
other agents. One second, he's telling me to pack my
bags, and then to standby the next minute. You know I
hadn't thought about it until now, but he could be
testing my stress levels; he is certainly working my

nerves. "Don't worry you'll have something soon, I'm currently collecting data to ensure that I send you on the perfect mission," is what he keeps telling me. But there's no such thing as perfection. If things were perfect, there would be no missions. I enjoyed not being on assignment for the first three months, but now I'm over it. I am doing my best to not get anxious while waiting, so I have taken up archery and knife throwing to de-stress while I wait. Did I mention that I am teaching myself, and getting good at it? Oh wait, I just felt a buzz on my special phone, hopefully this will be M.E. with a mission assignment that I can accept. Let's see what the message says, because I am ready to go!

The Assignment

"P. W,

This new mission particularly aligns well with your previous experience. As it currently stands, more and more employees are starting to complain about issues in the workplace, and nothing else. Angry employees can be seen and heard in breakrooms, at water coolers, and after-hour venues talking about their problems, while solutions remain undeveloped. Not only are employees not enjoying themselves at work, but corrupt supervisors and managers are robbing companies blindly of their most valuable resources. Good people. There are others in the field right now trying to locate the root of this problem, and while some developments have been made, I think we will need to go deeper. We have learned that the majority of these complaints are being filtered into the location you will be sent to. Now, here is where things get interesting, you will also be infiltrating to discover why the employees of the location you are being sent to appear to be content to listen to complaints each day. You will be undercover as a regular employee, with no managerial duties or privileges, and no gadgets, so behave yourself. If I find out, and I will find out, that you were the initiator in any mishaps during this assignment, I will see to it that you retire there. Stay low, do your job, and return with the information that we need.

-M.E."

Well don't threaten me with a good time boss. *Really no gadgets? How does he expect me to endure THIS mission with no tools?* I feel the walls closing in on me now! I'll be chained to a desk and forced to sit and listen, and listen, and LISTEN to people complain all day. He knows I need mobility! I like to flow; I need movement! You will never guess the name of this company either. They call themselves "WeCare Reporting Line," which is really the response to the name of last company I was on assignment for called "Who Cares Complaint Line." This better not be the same company rebranded! One of these days I'm just going to smash this phone to pieces and walk away from it all! Doesn't he know that this mission could ruin me? Does he even care? And if that wasn't bad enough, I get a knock on my door shortly after reading the message and it's Makeba Hawks, the agency's costume director, in all her Kenyan splendor standing outside with a rolling rack for the wardrobe I'll be required to wear while on my mission. Seeing Makeba usually feels like Christmas came early because she and I both love to play dress up, but not this time. I should have known something was up when Makeba's excitement did not match mine. She usually greets me with a mile long smile, and says "Hello my favorite baby doll," but now her smile is a kept secret. "Before you explore, just keep in mind that this new assignment calls for you to blend in a little differently than usual Dear," Makeba cautioned me in her Kenyan accent. "Well technically I'm different for each mission Hawks," I responded in a cheery tone. I could not wait to unveil my new wardrobe and was already imagining how fly I was about to be. I felt like the celebrities do when Beyonce sends them a new Ivy Park release. "M.E. just assigned me to a crappy mission, I should at least be able to look g-," I paused in mid-sentence because I refused to believe the atrocity that stood before me. "What is this?" I could not believe my eyes; hanging on the rolling garment rack was a combination of red, blue, white, and black polo shirts, with – "Those are khakis," Makeba responded meekly. I was mortified. "So basically, he wants me to be Jake from State Farm!" Scratch that, I was livid. "No gadgets, no lead role, no fashions, what's next, will I ride a moped to get to work? Makeba chuckled before replying, "Luckily Nick Sparrow was able to talk him out of doing that, these are for you." Makeba handed me two sets of car keys. "She's parked outside." I knew better than to get my hopes up this time and considering that M.E. was talked out of making me ride to work on a moped, I should be grateful. I stepped outside the front door to the black minivan that awaited me. "M.E. suggested that you also get close enough to some of your future new co-workers and felt that carpooling may be a good idea to do from time-to-time." I started to massage my temples, because this could not be happening to me, things were going downhill fast. "Well at least it has a sunroof," I mustered the strength to say. I quickly needed to locate the silver lining in this situation, since there was no rainbow or pot of gold. "Aw cheer up love, M.E. really wants you to be able to concentrate on this new assignment and felt that the less attention you got for your glamour and fancy cars the better." My face showed confusion and Makeba could read it well. Although I have driven some very sexy cars in the past, I have never flaunted them to anyone and besides they were part of the job. "Oh Dear, M.E. didn't tell you, did he?" She knew she had sparked my curiosity, "Tell me about what?" "I shouldn't have opened my mouth, but it's only fair that I tell you now." My ears were twitching, because it was unlike M.E to not make me privy to every detail regarding an assignment, especially if my identity and safety could be compromised. "Well, do you remember your last mission?" I never forget a mission, not even the ones I would prefer to. "Of course I do. It was when I was sent to-" Makeba stopped me mid-sentence, "No need to mention it Dear, we all remember, but it was the custom Maserati that drew in the attention and almost did you in." I had been issued a sleek Gran Turismo and had chosen the color black, you know for subtlety. "But Makeba, you've got to admit the 'Rati was a hard act to follow." I named "him" Midnight because he was so still and quiet. Makeba nodded her head in agreement, because she was the one that suggested the red interior with shiny black accents for Midnight. "It was and then you became hard to *not* follow because of it too Dear." Makeba allowed her words to sink in before she continued. "And you also became the most privately searched person on Google by your coworkers." Makeba revealed to me that the people from my previous assignment became so intrigued by how I was able to do the job I was performing and

8

afford that type of car to drive. M.E. discovered from tapping into their personal devices and conversations that they had arranged for their friends and some family members to have me followed, ambushed, and robbed. I had a feeling that something else was amiss during that time because M.E. started sending me instructions to take specific routes when leaving "work". Luckily, no one had discovered the fortress I had been assigned to live in. I never questioned M.E. instructions, only did as told. "Yes, he placed demolition agents on those special routes to ensure your safety and to also "intervene" on your behalf just in case." Now, my wheels were spinning. "So no one was hurt in the three car pile-up on Walters Avenue, right?" Makeba was delighted that the light bulb had finally switched on. "No Dear, but the two vehicles that were tailing you did get totaled." I was stunned to realize that the car wreck had been orchestrated to protect me. Moments like those, made me believe M.E. would make a great protective husband in real life, despite him being the occasional thorn in my side.

Makeba's shocking revelation explained why I found everyone to be so nosy on that assignment. They were always extra friendly, but every conversation felt like interviews, some even felt like interrogations. "M.E. really thought it would be a good idea to strip me of my drip to not have people being extra curious about me, you know this is almost as bad as him assigning me to work in prison right?" "Oh dear, let's not ever revisit those moments as they were not your finest." Makeba had a point on that one. "Deal", But why me 'Keba! I know there's a recruit eager to prove themselves." I could tell I was starting to wear on Makeba's nerves, but she knew what she was risking by bringing these God-awful clothes to me. "Dear, you already know the answer to that question; your previous experiences will especially serve this mission." Yeah Right! Bosses will butter you up like a biscuits, when they know they are about to make you do something you DO NOT want to do. The reality of this new mission was draining the life out of me before I even started it. I decided that my "real" mission would be to get in and out of WeCare

Reporting Line as soon as possible. "Come dear, have a look," Makeba took my hand as she guided me back to the wardrobe rack. She sensed that I needed a boost. "I left a box for you in the back corner, take a look inside." I was pleasantly surprised and speechless. "You wear this on the last day of your assignment." Makeba had lowered her voice and was looking around as if it were not just the two of us inside. "No, he doesn't know that I snuck this for you, and it won't hurt him to find out about it when you make your grand exit," she said anticipating my question. I grabbed Makeba into a bear hug. "Makeba, I should have never doubted you." Makeba smoothed out her clothes once I released her, and said "and don't you ever do it again, I have to be going now, send me a pic of what you wear on your first day." I walked her out front where a driver awaited her in a black Cadillac Escalade with two motorcycles trailing behind it. She blew me an air kiss before settling into the backseat. I looked on in amusement as I watched my friend, "the queen of all things grand," make her exit. Makeba's surprise had slightly lifted my spirits, but that was hours ago. Now I'm back in my feelings and need to exhale. Let's chat later.

Day One

---o---

The next morning, I awake to the birds chirping on my phone. It was show time. I reviewed the details of my character, so that I would not step out of line. I prayed, ate breakfast, worked out, showered and got dressed. I decided to wear the black polo with khakis since technically I was still in mourning. I grabbed my lunch tote, and my other tote, that contained no gadgets, my keys and headed to the minivan. I refuse to give this "block with wheels" a name. I settled inside, started the ignition and was on my way. I rode in silence, as I knew these would be my last moments of quiet and solace before entering the chaotic world of complaining. I found a park for the minivan, then stepped out. My phone starts to buzz and the words, "Looking good -M.E." flash across the screen before disappearing. As expected, M.E. was somewhere watching me to make sure that my attire was "appropriate", otherwise, I would have been directed to one of the hidden lock boxes that contained a change of clothes. M.E. stays 10 steps ahead of everybody. I showed up on time according to my assignment, and not my actual work schedule. M.E had instructed that I intentionally show up to work late from time-to-time as well, because he thought being late would allow me to blend in.

I used my code to clock in and find Oliver, my manager, who did not seem to mind that I am late. "Don't worry about it sweetheart, I'm just glad that you got here and that you're safe." His voice was so calm and fatherly. I almost thought he was going to pull me into a warm hug and kiss me on my forehead. Oliver acted as if he genuinely cared that I had made it. He stepped away from me and got my coworkers' attention. "Everybody she's here, now let's show her our best WeCare Welcome." My coworkers arose from their seats all at once. I stood there like a deer in headlights. I didn't know if I should stay or run for the hills. *What had M.E. gotten me into?* I was starting to feel that WeCare Reporting was really an occult masking itself to be a business. *What's was up with these people standing up at the same time like that?* They better not expect me to do that for the next person they hire. He pointed me in the direction of my station where I was stopped by each person that I walked past and given a "Welcome" trinket. I was completely caught off guard, but took the kind gestures in stride. They all watched me get to my desk, and sat down only after I had. This place was different and interesting. After their welcome initiation, I found myself completely comfortable in this atmosphere, and although we were responsible for taking complaints, the center itself radiated positivity. I got set up and waited to take my first call. It was a slow morning because the only calls I received were from people who were asking for department telephone numbers, or to be transferred to different departments. As the day wore on, I became more antsy once I started to experience withdrawals brought on by a lack of action. I could really use a shot of adrenaline. I also noticed that my co-workers did not seem to be freaking out much before or after their calls. With barely any calls coming in, I decided to take an early lunch break. I settled on sitting in the back corner of the breakroom to observe its incoming and outgoing traffic. I took a sip of water after each bite of my dry turkey sandwich, M. E's idea of course, and pondered how the remainder of my day would be. My thoughts were interrupted when Shannon, one of the managers, approached me. "How's it going Hun, how did you like our warm welcome?" During the interview, I pinpointed her to be the most empathetic out of all the managers I met on the panel. Each time she asked me a question during the interview, I felt that she was finding a way to connect to my response. "I'm doing quite well, and yourself?" I decided not to acknowledge the second part of her question because the jury was still out on that one. I was eager to hear her response because I had been in the process of drafting notes on the company before she came in. That was my fault, usually I'm allowed to have lunch in a private space , i.e. my car, but M.E. suggested that I take occasional breaks in the break room, to give the appearance of being approachable. "It's been awfully slow this morning, but we are hopeful that things will pick up." Shannon continued to explain that the more calls that come in, the more money comes in for everyone. "*Everyone?*" This intrigued me, it is not every day that you hear about a company sharing its wealth with their employees. I needed to know more. "Oh yes Hun, it is one of the ways we try to show our appreciation for you being here and staying committed to the work that we do." Shannon said that Mario and Shawn, the CEOs, knew that our work was stressful, so they found unique ways, in addition to the traditional ones to show staff appreciation. "We won't pizza party you to death around here, honey. We do that too, but we're more creative than that." Shannon began to share more about the unique team building outings the company had treated their staff to. "We'd love to have you at our next 'Karoake and Wings' if you're interested, I do a mean rendition of Bodak Yellow." I almost choked on air because Shannon struck me as more of a "Baby One More Time" karaoke performer, but either way I would definitely be present at the next function. I now understood why no one seemed to be on edge earlier. Although this was my first day on the job, it still felt as if the company was trying to earn me. Shannon allowed me to enjoy the remainder of my break in peace. The pace had picked up when I returned, and I was able to get a little action.

" Who do I need ta talk to about settin' this jackhole straight?" I spoke to a gentleman by the name of George who revealed that the next time his manager, Matthew, yelled at him in front of his coworkers, he planned to leave the print of his right hand on the left side of Matthew's face. "I'm telling you now, he needs to figure out how'da talk ta me soon because if he don't I plan to rattle his brain." I was immediately grateful that George had not been my first call of the day. I frequently used the "mute" button to avoid George hearing me laugh. His deep southern drawl put me in the mind of a cowboy ready to duel at high noon, and considering the context of our conversation, I guess he was. "Sir, I know that you are upset, but am I to believe that you intend to physically assault leadership?" I tried using a legal term or two because George would be going to jail if Matthew did not come at him the right way. "No, I don't want to assault him ma'am. I'm going to knock his innards outwards!" Either this was George's cry for help or his cry for war, but I had to at least persuade him to explore a few other options before resorting to violence. "Sir, have you spoken to HR about your problem? Does anyone know that you are upset about Matthew's actions towards you?" I got as much information about this issue as possible, because this company was literally about to have Matthew's innards on their hands. George admitted that he had not spoken to any other management about his feelings. I was lucky that the company had specific notes to instruct their staff to speak to them before reporting on the line. George assured me that he would take these steps. "Don't be surprised if you receive a collect call from the local county detention facility." George had made up his mind that he was going to jail should the company fail to solve his problem. I told George it would be my pleasure to accept the charges for his call to document the details of *that* report if it ever came to that happening. I took a few more calls that were not nearly as high strung as George's. I gathered my welcome gifts and left once the day was over.

I was hoping to not run into anyone else asking me what I thought about my first day on the job. I had answered that question at least 50 times. I purposely told one of my coworkers, Jared, that I hated the place, just for thrills. He looked as if he were ready to call an emergency intervention to convince me to change my mind. "I really thought you were serious," he said relieved to hear that I was just joking. "Oh no, it seems like a genuine place to be." I was expecting Jared to say something else, but then his eyes had become misty when I looked at him. He stepped into my personal space, looked me squarely in the eye, and said "This place has saved my life." His voice quivered when he spoke. He looked as if he wanted to say more, then decided against it. "See you tomorrow," he pat me on the shoulder and walked away. Now that was strike one because I decided to let them slide with that Welcoming initiation. I don't know what it was about this place, but Jared wasn't the only person that felt the way he did about WeCare Reporting. I'd heard the testimonials all day. I continued down the long hallway when something caught my attention. The door to one of the interview rooms was slightly ajar where I heard low humming, whispers, and meditative music. I quieted my steps and moved closer so that I could see. Inside were Oliver, Jared, and Mario, one of the CEOs and who was leading the exercise, were sitting Indian style on the ground in a dimly lit room. They repeatedly said "I am safe. I have transformed. Nothing can hurt me." I stepped away from the door in sheer confusion. "Safe from what?," I wondered. That was definitely strike two. One more flash of crazy, and I'm out for good.

Months Later

Today was just one of *those* days. I'm not even sure Monica, at twelve-years-old, could even begin to write about this type of day, but maybe Brandy could while sitting up in her room. Relax, that was just a little Versuz humor. I was only kidding. Can't you tell that I'm a little delirious? I know I sound like I completely hate my "job," which could not be further from the truth. WeCare Reporting Line is great, and I am enjoying it more than what I thought I would; but work today was nothing short of a circus. I see why my coworker, Sheila purposely hung up on her caller by accident, so that she could get home at a decent hour. Sheila, I saw what you did, but your secret is safe with me. Whew, what a day! You read the note, so you know what's going on. I'm currently on "assignment" to document corporate complaints for several companies. This assignment is panning out to be more successful than expected. With all the calls coming in, it has become apparent why employees feel the way they do about their employers. The people were calling the center in droves today, and we could barely keep up! My guess is that an employee from every company we service had something they wanted to complain about today. We had taken 1,000 calls by noon, just to give you an idea of how deep it got in the trenches. All of a sudden, the center goes black while I'm in the process of wrapping up my conversation with a gentleman who reported seeing Facebook photos of his coworker, who was supposed to be out on FMLA, enjoying the sun and fun on a beach. My first thought was that M.E. had sent Nick Sparrow to create a diversion to break me out, but instead a spotlight shoots to Oliver. "Ladies and Gentlemen, let's give a round of applause to Lucca because he's just taken the 1,000th call of the day." The next thing I know, a disco ball descends from the ceiling and the spotlight is placed on Lucca, who looks just as confused as I did on my first day. *BBHMM* by Rihanna starts playing from the speakers, and then

Oliver and Shannon go make it rain dollar bills on Lucca. His confusion immediately changed to delight after being awarded $1,000 on-the-spot. I have to admit the impromptu celebration was a pleasant surprise, but then it was back to work as usual. "Who knows, if we're lucky we'll give another grand away," Oliver said before everything resumed back to normal. The levels of complaints I heard ranged from petty to felonious. The phones would not stop ringing, and people could not stop talking, at length, about their work problems. It was so bad, I started to hyperventilate, then had to pretend that I was having an asthma attack because if M.E. finds about it, he will start planning for me to retire from that place. Luckily, I found the asthma pump I used on another assignment, because if management had notified my emergency contact person (M.E.), I would be one thoroughly cooked bird, but I digress. Now, about this tornado of a day...

I even had an angry parent to call in to talk about how horrible their children's workplace had been towards them. I am not joking, and I am not talking about the parents of teenagers either. Ms. Gladys had THE audacity to report that her son, Jason's job had given him a written warning for being repeatedly late to work. *First of all, Ms. Gladys, Jason is very much a grown man with bills, and if you are not trying to be his financier, you need to mind your business. Secondly, Jason needs to stop telling you his business, because your level of "Mama Bearing" and "sMothering" inspires those movies on Lifetime. Thirdly, when I asked Ms. Gladys if Jason had been getting to work late, she said, "Well no more than 15 to 20 minutes." Bye Gladys! Jason is about to lose his job because of you.*

I took my time with my last call because I was determined for THAT call to be my LAST call for the day. After I wrapped up the report, I was out! I took a different exit when I left today too, just in case Mr. Oswald tried to hold me up talking about what happened... "This day in black history," he wants to be Morgan Freeman sooooo bad. I started to hear low murmurings of management possibly needing staff to work overtime before I left. I was certain that I would not be going above and beyond the call of duty today. I had conducted enough research and it was time for me to go home. I moved at lightning speed getting out of there. I plan for us to get more acquainted once I'm settled at home. I'll tell you more about myself, and a few other things that have been on my mind lately; but right now I want to ride in silence with the sunroof opened on "Ms. Mini" (yes, I named the minivan), so that I can air out all of this toxic energy absorbed from listening to people complain all day. Ciao.

30 minutes later

Welcome home to me! I'm just here sipping my ginger tea with a hint of something extra from my favorite "Fearless" mug, in a Snuggies on my favorite side of the couch.

I know it seems like every time we come across each other's paths that I am either in a rush or a bad mood, but that is not always who I am. I promise. Allow me to introduce myself, my name is Phoenix Washington. No, that is not my club name, it's more of a stage name for my line of work, which leads me to why my work is referred to as an assignment or mission, and not a job. My actual job sends me on different assignments to carry out classified missions. I have fulfilled many roles over the course of my time with the "agency." At any point I can be a nanny, a driver, a stylist, a model, a boss--it just depends on what duty calls for. Who knows, we may have even worked together at some point. My latest assignment has landed me at a call center where I listen to multiple complaints day in and day out which sounds like a drag, but my boss could not think of a more clever way for me to "plant" myself into the company, so here we are. While not revealing too much about the entire assignment, my job is to infiltrate, educate, and evacuate in order to share my findings with everyone on the team. I cannot wait for the evacuation part. Trust me, it takes me forever to wash off the stench of negativity every day, but until that day comes, I'll purge myself with you.

The Rise And Fall Of Phoenix

I still remember the day I was recruited into the L.I.F.E. Agency. I was younger and more naive, which made me the perfect candidate. The less experience you have to start with, the better, and it remains that way until this day. The interview process was similar to how many of us ended up working at fast food chains as teenagers, I showed up to the interview and got the job. Naturally, I have liked some assignments better than others, but every mission has been accomplished. Knowledge and information are the most valued currencies within the agency and is what determines each agents' next assignment at L.I.F.E. I have witnessed some of my comrades be promoted to high-level agents, who now issue assignments. Some receive a high ranking within their next assignment, some have already retired, while some are relocated to repeat the same assignment in a different setting. I am definitely the latter with this current assignment, but my previous knowledge is making it a piece of cake to perform. I'm still not crazy about hearing people complain all day, but at least I was not assigned to return to the same place I initially gained the experience from.

I have been assigned to assume the role of a Risk Specialist, which does not require me to be an expert in employee relations or human resources, so much as it requires for me to act as a bridge of communication to express employee grievances to their employers. How it works is that disgruntled employees call into the contact center to report the issues they are experiencing in the workplace. I interview them to obtain more details about the issue and submit a report for their respective companies to review. Simple in the grand scheme, but after hearing some of their stories, I am convinced the devil is literally in the details. Some of the bosses to these employees had to be manufactured in Satan's sweatshop. There is no other way to explain their debauchery.

Employees feel a sense of safety when speaking to a neutral party about how badly they feel about their work lives. They unload their souls to me, and I document every pertinent detail for the company to know about. This assignment requires me to be a traitor of sorts, a double agent (a triple agent in my case), if you will; however it's been through the trials and tribulations of disgruntled employees that I was awakened to the true nature of how people choose to act or not act to address conflict and concerns within their workplace environment.

After completing the L.I.F.E. Agency academy, one of my early assignments included me being an operations manager for a now defunct luxury valet company we'll call "Luxurious Parking." I started with Luxurious Parking while in the academy, then got promoted after graduating. I will not lie, I was hoping for a more exciting position with the government, since I had clearly "paid my dues." But what became clear was that

I had not paid enough. I had to experience the growing pains of hating where I was at that time in my life, but it being all I had for the moment. Eventually, I started to move up. No truer words were spoken when it was said that every level of elevation requires a more refined and defined version of yourself. In management, I was put to the task of terminating co-workers that I started with in order to tailor my vision of excellence. I also learned the difference between being cutthroat towards staff versus being cutthroat towards the issues sometimes created by staff, which at times were one in the same. I went from loathing Jet, the boss of Luxurious Parking, to developing a healthy level of respect for him. Unknown to me at the time, but these growing pains had been staged by design. I did not think much of him when I first started, but once I moved up the ranks of that assignment, I was exposed to some of the chess moves Jet made to keep us all in the game. I went from clocking in and clocking out by the hour to being salaried and "flewed out" City Girl style to visit potential work sites to grow and develop.

And then the assignment was pulled from me, but by that I time I was exhausted and simply happy to have freedom and a peace of mind within arm's reach. I won't lie, the severance helped a lot to ease the disappointment of no longer working a job that I had grown tired of doing. Matlock and Monk became "bae" during the period of me waiting for my next assignment from the agency.

My experiences in management made me confident in my abilities to grow and develop a team to be successful at any projected goal. I found myself seeking vacancies within the agency that would allow others to benefit from my encouragement. I came across one vacancy posting dealing in ethics and compliance. The assignment wanted potential candidates to act as employee support for various corporations. I wanted this one. I just knew I was a perfect fit; and had started to envision how proud I would make the agency with the work I would perform in this role. I was convinced that employees would start to flourish and blossom from my planted seeds of encouragement. I was trying to be a workplace fairy godmother, but just didn't know it at the time. I was too excited when Who Cares Complaint Line expressed interest in my joining their team as a Communication Specialist.

I must really give credit to Sherry, the woman who recruited me because after speaking to her, there was no other place for me to be. Sherry was good at what she did. Sherry was your favorite recruiter's favorite recruiter. The G.O.A.T. That woman could sell hell to the devil and he would use its fire as a down payment, so be wary of Sherry at the crossroads. I started with Who Cares Complaint Line in March of 2014, completed two weeks of training, then Boom! I found myself smack dab on the west side of hell. It did not take long for me to hate the Who Cares Complaint Line, but by the time it took me to realize that I had been hoodwinked and bamboozled, Sherry the charlatan, was gone in the wind. Who Cares Complaint Line was the only assignment that I came close to aborting. I loathed this assignment so much that my body started to reject going to this job on its own. I remember waking up one morning, and I could not walk! Can you imagine! I still had feeling in my legs, which were in excruciating pain. My doctor ended up writing me out of work for stress and ordered me to kick my feet up for the next seven days. Sherry, it is on sight if I ever see you again. I was innocent and you did not have to trick me the way that you did. I still have minor trust issues because of that woman. I roasted in the eternal fires of the Who Cares Complaint Line for approximately two years. I was so jaded by the time I left that place, but learned many valuable lessons from the experience; which is one reason I was specifically called for my current assignment. I vowed to never return to this line of work ever again, but as the saying goes…That's right, I'm in the same line of duty all over again, but will be approaching the assignment from a refreshed perspective.

It's a Different World

There's so much to say about the topic that I want to get into without knowing where to start, so here it is. The workplace, and I'll just drop the mic right now because you already know we are about to get into some real professional gangsta ish. In most cases, your job is a far cry from what you thought it would be like after graduating, or what the hiring manager sold it to be during the interview. Shows like *Girlfriends*, *Living Single*, and *A Different World* had us eager for the same success the writers created for Khadijah James, Kyle Barker, Maxine "The Maverick" Shaw, and Joan Clayton (Thank God for *Insecure*, because the struggle to the top is really real). Now I am not saying those levels of success are unattainable, it just won't look like what it did on T.V. When dealing in any professional or work setting, you should be observing from a lens with high definition versus your rose-colored ones.

Trust me, observing the real will also save you the disappointment of your expectations not being met in certain areas, and helps you to adjust more strategically. In HD, you will immediately notice the difference between Stephanie in marketing grinning or gritting her teeth at you every time you walk by. I once had this older gentlemen, Mr. Johnson, I believe his name was, tell me, "The friendliest dog will grin at you right before it bites you." #Bars. I do not remember what Mr. Johnson's profession was, but I remembered he carried himself as if he were a big deal, and he loved my smile. He may have been a dentist, come to think of it. That jewel of wisdom remained with me because number one, teeth can be used as weapons; and number two, some smiles serve as tools of deception. So, remember your perspective in HD equals reality, and a rose-colored perspective equals reality T.V.

Every organization has a standard for professionalism; interpretations may vary, yet standards still exist for the purpose of providing guidelines of how employees should conduct themselves while at work. It's like a script and your job title defines the role you play during the performance of your duties. Sound familiar? Standards of professionalism also exist to not only ensure that you can do the work you're being paid to produce, but that you also play nice while doing so.

And therein lies the problem. Playing nice at work is a long exhausting con game in the workplace. A person plays nice for 8 hours Monday through Friday, which is 40 hours a week, until playing nice gets played out. This reminds me of a meme my friend Allison sent me of a red demon relaxing in a hot bath with its human suit on the ground, a lit candle, and a glass of wine. The caption said, "Me after a long day of pretending to like people." Faking it to make it throughout the day added with a few people who display symptoms of having "ism and ness" (racism, ageism, sexism, pettiness, and b***hness) blends the perfect cocktail for a toxic workplace on the rocks. People placed in positions of leadership become intoxicated by power, and abuse their authority by isolating and mistreating their subordinates, because, who gon' check them? These managers who enjoy all-expense paid ego trips continue pulling the strings and plugs on the careers of the powerless and naïve.

Mergers and acquisitions spring forth new management that carry different views of how you complete your duties as an employee. Oftentimes "new" in the workplace does not always mean "better," and if said "new" management, supervisor, or team lead displays symptoms of having any of the aforementioned "isms and ness," then the work environment has transformed into a ruthless game of survival of the fittest. People become a lot less capable of playing nice under stress, which is a revealer of true character.

When this happens, many will try to rise to the occasion of gaining favor with the new leadership; but when that attempt fails, who do you run to? HR seems to be the most logical option because they know the organization's rules and policies, and how they should be applied. But what happens when they side with the ops after you have poured your heart out to them and asked for help? Does your will to fight go into overdrive, and if so, at what cost? Really, who has the constant energy to battle management, coworkers, and HR, while doing the job you are being paid for? More power to you if you do, but for how long? Let us not forget the importance of maintaining your mental and physical health as well.

Many of us are guilty of telling ourselves that we are strong, which equates to being built for the bullcrap, yet I beg to differ. Being strong should equate to you taking that bull by the horns and make him think twice about crapping anywhere near you. The strength we pride ourselves on makes us nothing more than well-paid and glorified doormats. It has become free advertisement for what you are willing to accept to not get fired. This "strength" is cosigned by fear and will have you afraid to ask for a life jacket while you drown. You can resort to vices and venting, but unless you resort to a solution, you will continue to have the problem.

I have been exposed to quite a bit since being planted into the system, some of the stories I have heard will make your head spin, but there are lessons to be learned from it all. I do not think the people who call in to complain are completely sold on that part, but in time they will be. Now that I'm in place, hopefully you will be open to experiencing what it feels like to advocate for yourself and win on your terms. It's time we get you some power in the big rich town. Cue the music.

Disclaimer: In the stories that follow, names have been changed to protect the innocent, guilty, and otherwise. You may believe I am telling your story, when in truth I am merely sharing my experience.

You Have A Problem, So What?

Typically, when speaking to a disgruntled employee seeking to report their grievances, I notice they have become so fixated on the problem that they neglect the possibility of there being a solution to it. Negativity wins marathons from the energy fed into it, *and* Redbull endorsements.

Not only do disgruntled employees believe they have a problem, but they also overlook certain resources in favor to speak to me about the problem. The business of negativity yields extremely high profit margins. Don't believe me? What dominates the headlines of most newspapers, magazines, and blogs besides Beyonce? Negativity. Put Beyonce's name in a scandal? Not only will the hive assemble and activate, but the internet traffic and sales increase, and whatever good happened in the world will get the corner pocket of the last page. I'll give you another example, while certain corporations have needed to downsize because of the pandemic, WeCare Reporting Line has been forced to increase staffing efforts in order to meet the demands of business. People make more time to complain, and focus on the problem, than they do for a solution. Many believe that solutions are the responsibility of the powers that be, which is the first indication of them believing they have none to turn a situation around. An employee can speak for nearly an hour, about the coworker who said their shoes were ugly on April 1, 2014 (not an actual complaint), than they can about what should be done to resolve their issue.

Complaining for the sake of complaining is highly unproductive, but complaining in a group is even worse. You mean to tell me that a group of disenchanted individuals, who happened to be disenchanted for the same reason, cannot develop at least ONE solution to address the root of their disenchantment? So basically, if solving this one problem was a group project, everyone would get an "F." Allow me to set the scene for you. Person A links up with Person B and Person C to complain about it being cold in the building while standing next to the thermostat. All parties become so engrossed in their conversation that the thermostat is ignored. One person will piggyback the same talking point as the person before them. They will all stand there complaining and shivering in their circle of comfort. A few "Man, that's crazy(s)" will be peppered into the conversation for flavor, a couple rumors will be birthed, but no one will dare step outside the scope of the problem to activate or "turn on" the solution. My conversations with dissatisfied employees go the same way. I usually ask them who else they have spoken to about the issue, and most times it is another coworker, who is unwilling to go any further than complaining about the same problem. You may do the same thing; it is easy to fall into the trap without realizing.

"She always has something negative to say about me, and I'm tired of it," was typically the way Katrina, an old friend, would start our conversation about how much she despised her boss, Helen. At one point, Katrina would contact me daily to tell me the theatrics of her day. Not only was Helen a dictator, but she also engaged in shady business. It seemed to Katrina that Helen scrutinized every detail of her existence. "Today, she told me that my braids were too little for the size of my head! Why would she say that? Does that mean I have a big head?," she asked one day. Most of her stories were hilarious because Katrina was over the top dramatic and comical. While the commentary was thoroughly entertaining, it did not change the fact that Katrina had an unresolved issue. If Katrina stripped away the jokes and the theatrics, the problem remained standing alone by itself with no possible solutions, because none were being developed. Katrina could spend hours talking about the problem, but the solution? Not so much. When I pointed out the fact that she was always complaining about the same thing; she told me that I did not understand what she was going through, and that she just wanted to vent. But that was it; she just wanted to vent. Katrina was not interested in taking action. She placed more power in the problem, than she did in her ability to solve it.

When you set your focus to seeking a solution, you realize that the problem is really a solution waiting to be discovered. In Katrina's scenario, Helen was mistreating her and engaging in questionable activities in front of her. Had Katrina realized her power to address Helen, she would have created a number of solutions, and getting hush money- I mean a raise would have been at the top of that list. Instead of being flustered on the phone with me, she could have directed her energy into a conversation with Helen. Katrina's feelings towards Helen disrespecting her were valid, but she had yet to discuss the issue with Helen. Very rarely does an employee initiate a "come to Jesus" with the offending party, so that boundaries can be established. We were humans long before we learned to be professionals, and some, more than others, lack a sense of awareness. It would be okay for Katrina to give Helen the benefit of the doubt and talk to her about how she made her feel. Saying something to the effect of, "Helen, the harsh tone and the comment you made about the size of my head and my hairstyle made me feel upset, (Suge Knightish), and undervalued." The conversation would be uncomfortable, but she was already feeling that way. By addressing the disrespect, Katrina could have created a space for awareness, presented the other party with the opportunity to change their behavior towards her, and have lightened her own load. Helen would know where she stood in terms of showing respect, and any failure to follow through would reflect her choices, but not Katrina's failure to communicate. Do the math, one problem yielded three solutions, four if she pursued the raise.

Chapter Check

1. Do I really have a problem if I am unwilling to address it?

2. Do I lack the tools and resources necessary to resolve the conflict?

3. Was the offense blatant, or should I investigate more to rule out the possibility?

Speak (up) Now or You will Never Be at Peace

Timing is another important element to consider when putting a rude supervisor, manager, or co-worker on notice for being unprofessional towards you. While it is never too late to stand up for yourself, you do not want to delay asserting yourself for too long. Unless you know that you can instantly address an issue with a composed demeanor, give yourself enough time to fully process the incident. Your reactionary time is pivotal for several reasons. Even the Bible tells you to be slow to anger. For starters, we are less likely to care what comes out of our mouths when we are angry and words have lasting effects. Think of how many people struggle as adults because of damaging comments made to them as children. The other reason is witnesses. Witnesses can be an asset to you when you address an issue with composure. A witness does not carry the obligation of choosing a party to side with, and will say what they saw without conviction.

Taylor's Story

Taylor called to report that she had been written up for unprofessional behavior. As I obtained more information about the incident, I learned that Taylor, who worked as a CNA, had been involved in a negative encounter with Leslie, a nurse, at the nursing home they both worked for. Taylor said that Leslie had rudely ordered her to complete a task, while she was in the middle of helping another resident. Taylor said she told Leslie that she would complete the task after helping the resident. "Right after I tell her that, she said, "F**k you, you don't talk to me that way!" Taylor never mentioned the tone she had used with Leslie to incite the response she received, but said that after being cursed at, she responded to Leslie in the same manner. "I said well f**k you too b***h," and rightly so because Leslie violated. Secretly, I was delighted to hear that

Taylor stood up for herself and was not going to just accept the disrespect, but her approach worked against her because there were witnesses. Unless they are being paid well to lie, or a family member is being held hostage *until* they lie, witnesses are only loyal to memory. If you show grace under fire, they will be impressed by your poise, but will be able to recall every single detail when you behave otherwise. The reason for this is because you did more to stimulate their senses. Had Taylor considered her surroundings before responding to Leslie, she may not have needed to report her issue because those witnesses would have worked in her favor. Yes, the witnesses could attest that Leslie was the instigator, but would have also told management that Taylor remained calm. Taylor could have walked away, and the witnesses would only be able to report that much on her behalf, and also empathize with her need to remove herself from the incident to gain perspective. Some may have even offered Taylor support by completing what Leslie had initially asked her to do. Taylor could have even held her composure long enough to have a supervisor be present to address Leslie's actions. Even if she still responded, selecting a better choice of words paired with an authoritative tone, would have been better than responding the way that she did. Why? Witnesses. Had Taylor evacuated her angry place a little sooner, she would have realized, "I can use this audience to my advantage," but unfortunately, Taylor got in the mud with a pig and guess what happened?

"They gave me a final written warning for unprofessional behavior in front of residents and staff," Taylor really seemed confused on how that happened, but I wasn't. And I know you are probably thinking that's not fair, Leslie should have gotten a warning too because she started it, but such is life, especially in the workplace. What saved Leslie is the fact that she was a nurse and Taylor was a CNA. If the going ever got tough and budget cuts needed to be made in the form of labor reduction, Taylor's position is the more disposable one. A nurse can still perform their medical duties and CNA duties if it ever came to that, but a

CNA could not perform a nurse's duties legally. I mean no offense to any CNAs out there; you all are REAL MVPs to me. I believe wholeheartedly you should be paid more just based on all that you experience in many facilities from sexual harassment from residents, being physically assaulted, to inappropriate slurs directed at you, nurses mistreating you, and the occasional lack of support from management. You are appreciated. Now, back to my point. Although she was dead wrong for how she conducted herself in front of fellow coworkers and residents, Leslie is "viewed" as the more valued employee. My sixth sense tells me that Leslie knew this as well. Taylor stood up for herself, as she should have, but she allowed emotions to overshadow strategic calculation. If you stick around, I'll tell the story about the woman that got "disposed of" in a similar scenario in another chapter.

Alexandria's Story

Alexandria was a nurse who found herself in a similar predicament, but her issue was with two fellow nurses,

Pamela and Julie. Alexandria explained that she believed Pamela and Julie were responding to her with sarcasm on numerous occasions. "They are always saying, I find it funny how this, and I find it funny how that, whenever I am in the process of another duty when they need something done." I will also mention that Alexandria disclosed to me that she was of a different nationality, so she did not have a command of common American phrases and expressions. Alexandria told me that because of this fact she would never respond to Pamela and Julie's commentary because she was unsure how to respond, until one day, "I just told them to shut up! I was tired of it. I was preparing to start medication rounds, when they asked me to search for a medical record they could search for themselves!" Alexandria's fuse had blown. I silently cheered for her on the other end of the line because she did not allow a language barrier to confuse her intuition. "Pamela turned to Julie and said, I just find it funny how, and that was it," Alexandria said as she recounted the incident that led her to calling me that day. Just like with Taylor, I was happy that Alexandria did not allow her co-workers to isolate her and she stood up for herself, but now she was worried! Pamela and Julie accused her of being rude, but she took them to task for their previous actions that led to how she chose to address them. The difference between Taylor and Alexandria is that Alexandria took time to confirm the suspicions of her co-workers treating her with sarcasm. She didn't react immediately also because Pamela and Julie were more underhanded with their actions, where Leslie was bold. Alexandria was also at an advantage. Because English was not her first language, she had the ability to effectively communicate with patients of a different demographic. Alexandria was more of an asset in this regard and had probably been hired by her company because of her multilingual abilities, along with her qualifications. Alexandria also escalated the incident through the proper channels within her workplace and obtained support from her leaders. She was afraid that her actions would reflect poorly on her later, either way

Pamela and Julie now knew to be strictly professional when speaking to Alexandria.

The other side of this coin are those who say nothing at all, out of fear, and still get the short end of the stick. Employees who report being wrongfully terminated fall into this category. They tell me about how long they have been with a company, when they started being treated poorly, when they realized they were being targeted for termination, and some of the blatantly disrespectful things that were said to them. I have spoken to more than a handful of people who have taken verbal lashings. One guy told me that his manager had become comfortable with referring to him as "fatso" in front of his peers. He should have channeled his inner "George." Others have dealt with the value of their contributions being diminished, but they took the abuse because they were afraid to lose their jobs and not be able to provide for their families. What's interesting is that this fear to speak up in an effort to not lose a job rarely ever works. People still get the ax despite remaining silent, and find themselves in the eye of the storm they feared; caught up in a whirlwind of unsettled emotions and weighed down from carrying the burden of words unspoken. I believe that in hindsight, they start to recall all the chances they had to speak up for themselves, missing 100% of the shots they did not take. Cold world.

Note: Know when to speak and how to speak up for yourself. Some of your most "gangsta" moves will include a hint of calculated class.

Chapter check

1. Am I okay with someone else accurately recalling my actions or repeating my words?

2. Am I able to effectively express my grievance to the offending party?

3. Should a third party become involved when I address this problem?

4. Who is my audience?

Deflection is a Reflection

eflection Anyone? Nobody does deflection better than politicians and lying celebrities. Wait! They're the same people! When I take calls from employees, who are in fact guilty of what they were reprimanded for, they usually display difficulty responding to close-ended (yes or no) questions because they do not want to focus on the acts committed so much as they want to explain what justified the act. These are among some of my favorite types of calls to take since I enjoy the challenge of getting them to acknowledge that they are the root of their own problem. Such callers are angry and disgruntled for a different reason. They are upset about being caught and need to act quickly to preserve their hide or, CYB (cover your butt). Most of their anger is hot air sprinkled with a lack of self-awareness. They will call about being mistreated, but once we start unpacking the issue, it turns out they were just upset about being addressed or called out for causing the issue. Remember Ms. Gladys? She and her son Jason dominate this category. Apparently, Jason was too upset to speak for himself, so Ms. Gladys did what she felt had to be done. "I need to report Paper and Plastics for discrimination and harassment, they just wrote my son up for being late!" Ms. Gladys's energy was a bit much for the hour that she called, but she told me she'd just spent an hour talking to Jason about it, so calling the line was her next phase in the pursuit of workplace justice. I say, "Okay ma' am, so your son's warning was act of discrimination due to tardiness?" She was adamant that her answer was Yes, and that I had understood her correctly. Doing my best to gently poke the bear, I asked what other company actions taken against Jason led her to believe he was being discriminated against aside from his tardiness. "Well, they gave him a verbal about it two weeks ago," which did not answer my question at all. I pressed a little more because nothing about what she reported screamed that Uncle Jesse Jackson or Al Sharpton needed to be contacted. Not once did she mention race, gender, religion, nationality or a disability as the reason Jason was being handled in the manner that he was, so I asked her the million dollar question, "Well has he been late ma'am?" "Jason drives the 2001 Toyota Corolla that his father and I purchased for him when he graduated, and he's just now starting to have problems with the starter. On top of that, he has to make at least three detours because of all the work being done on the roads to his regular route to work." Gladys' responses were starting to make me think she was having an extra conversation on the side while speaking to me, because I know I did not ask her anything about the kind of car that Jason drove, but I responded, "Yes, I hear that Toyota's are a very supreme brand, but I believe I just asked you if Jason has been getting to work late." She knew the answer to the question when I initially asked, but she also knew the truth of her answer would instantly deflate her ballooned allegations. There was a pregnant pause before she said, "Yes." I decided to add insult to injury and ask her "Did Jason get the write up for being late today?" "There was a lot of heavy rain today where we are, and we've always told Jason to be careful and drive slowly in the rain." Gladys was not trying to incriminate her baby by any means, "So am I to assume that your answer to my question is also, yes?" Sometimes you have to roll with the punches during an investigative interview. Gladys knew I was holding her over the barrel now. Another slow "Yes" emerged from her mouth. I heard her take a deep breath as if she were trying to breathe new life into her beliefs that the company was discriminating against her son. "But he was no more than 15 to 20 minutes late." I heard a trace of triumph in her voice that should not have been there, "Ok ma'am was this 15 to 20 minutes today or the last time Jason was late?" I know she sensed my smirk. "Are you being funny right now?" Gladys was pulling at any straw that she could use. "No ma'am, simply trying to get a clear understanding of the issue, and relying on you to help me do that, is there a problem?"

Shannon gave me the "thumbs up" for my response because she was monitoring my call. "Oh no there's no problem at all," and Gladys reluctantly divulged that yes, Jason had been 15 to 20 minutes on the day he received the written warning for tardiness. I decided to put Gladys out of her misery and end the interview with her. "What resolution are you seeking for this reported matter, ma'am? As if she had rehearsed her response to this questions Gladys said, "Jason is a great boy, and the company should really just give him a chance, that's it." Nothing more needed to be discussed or justified. Gladys and Jason both allowed his car troubles, detours, and weather, to be excuses for why he could never be on time, but his bosses did not share the same sentiments. And as far as this "chance" Gladys needed the company to give Jason? The company had given him that chance every day, from Monday to Friday.

Bryan's Story

"Bryan, I'm sure you are aware of why I asked to speak with you today." That was me trying to sound so official. During my assignment with Luxurious Parking, I managed a guy named Bryan who made excuses for why he could never show up on time, just like Gladys did for Jason. He entered the office and took a seat. Bryan was our team's comedian, so to have him not making a joke let me know he would be taking our conversation seriously. My approach to the situation was for him to check my accountability to him as his manager." "Bryan, do you believe I do a decent job of making sure that you have the necessary tools that you need to perform your job in a timely manner?" "You're always on point with everything." Had I not already known that about myself, then I might have believed Bryan was trying to flatter me to get out of the conversation we were having, but he was right. I was incredibly determined to be an organized manager. After getting his confirmation that he agreed that I took accountability for my position in management, it was time to place him in the spotlight. "When you were offered the position, you were made aware of the shift you would be required to fill, right?" He seemed perplexed by the question but responded, "Yes." I pressed on with my next question, "Has your schedule changed since you've been here?" He replied with a confident "No." "So why can't you make it in on time? His world stopped. It was like he had never considered that him being late had become an issue. It took him a minute to recover. "Well I get off at 4 pm and don't get to bed until 11 or 12. I get up at 4:45 in the morning and on the road by 5:30," Bryan was scheduled to start work at 7 am, and his routine would have been fine had he not been battling Atlanta's traffic. To be fair, Atlanta's traffic is an uncompromising reality, so guess who needed to switch up their routine? Bryan. It became apparent that Bryan had issues with time management, but his issue had already started to affect the team's efforts, and people had started to complain. I issued him a written warning so that he understood the severity of the matter, but I decided to help him devise a plan. "Let's brainstorm some of the things you can do to shorten your prep time in the morning." Bryan and I spent the next 30 minutes developing ideas that could help him be on time. From the brainstorm, Bryan picked his top three favorite solutions which became his plan. "You're making this my plan; you think you're slick." Bryan was slowly morphing back into his comedic self. "Bryan you catch on quick," and we both laughed in unison. That day Bryan was officially in contract with himself to succeed or fail on his terms.

When you can take accountability for your actions whether you are in the right or not, you are certainly on your way to complaining less and working things out more. Accountability is a tool of the empowered.

Chapter Check

1. Am I the root of my own issue?

2. What actions can I take to be better in a similar situation?

3. What have I learned about myself from this incident?

Pick and Choose Wisely

Video games are not my thing, although I have enjoyed playing Super Mario and Mortal Kombat a time or two, but for the purpose of my next point, let's use Mortal Kombat as our example. Before the game starts, you have to select a character or player. You scroll the roster of characters and review their stats, which include their powers and capabilities. You start to play the game after you've chosen the character you like. Let's say that you choose the game's most powerful character to play with, but still lose. How did that happen? It's possible that a few things could have occurred, such as the right strategy not being applied to respond to the environment that you were fighting in. In my opinion, Shang Tsung would be the ideal character because of his ability to morph into other characters, which gives him access to his opponent's moves. It's possible that you lost playing with the most powerful player, because you did not study your opponent at all. Had you studied your opponent, you would know when and how to expose their weaknesses. More importantly, have you mastered your own powers? You're probably thinking, "Chill, it's just a game," but it gets that serious when you're playing to win. The workplace is no different. You, your co-workers, managers, supervisors, and HR department are all players in the company's game. You have roles and responsibilities that could be considered your powers. The lower your position is in rank, the least amount of power you have, seemingly. Like with the video game, your objective is to figure out what moves you should be making to win, especially when conflict exists. These next two scenarios were losing situations for the people involved because they failed to strategize and understand the opposition before being mastered by it.

Camille's Story

Do you Remember in Taylor's scenario when I mentioned that she probably got the worse end of the stick in her situation involving Leslie the nurse because she was a CNA, and if a critical situation occurred then Taylor would get the boot before Leslie did? Well Elise, who is also a CNA, cashed in her reality check when she got sent home for telling Nurse Camille that going forward, she needed to get her own box of gloves. "I was so confused, like all I said was in the future, you go get your own gloves. The next thing I know Camille says she won't work if I stay in the building and then Walter, the supervisor tells me that Monica, the DON was sending me home." Elise explained that in the 6 months of her working at the rehabilitation facility, no one had ever instructed her to go get gloves for them, nor was she informed that it was in her job description to do so. "I still don't even know if that's what the company wants me to do now." Elise had just finished responding to a resident, when Camille asked her to get the gloves. "She was just sitting there, not doing anything with a smirk on her face." I detected that

Camille and Elise did not like each other, so I asked. "Not really she tried to lie and say I was monitoring my coworker's lunch break and snitching back to the boss which was a lie, and I told them that while she stood there." Aha! So Camille's request had not been innocent at all yet a way to get under Elise's skin and it worked. Camille had also anticipated that Elise would have something to say about her request, which she planned to take advantage of. Camille was crafty; she studied her opponent, she mastered Elise's temperament, and created the perfect opportunity to strike. What I found even more interesting was that Camille was even able to make Monica bend to her will as well. "She told Walter to tell Monica, that either I leave or she would leave, but we both couldn't both be there." Camille was serpent wise and knew that if she applied just the right amount of pressure, she could leverage the power she had to get Monica, who had the most power and decision-making ability, to do what she wanted. Once Camille presented Walter and Monica with the ultimatum, it was Elise who got tossed and further proved that Camille was the real MVP. Camille knew the odds were in her favor the moment she made Monica choose her. Camille also realized that the higher up a person is in rank, the more they concern themselves with what is "best for business." She orchestrated a scenario that made her the most obvious choice. Even though she got her feelings hurt, Elise needed this scenario to play out the way it did. Hopefully, she was taking notes from her opponent.

Note: Opposition is one heck of a teacher.

Karen's Story

"I need to report a co-worker for being inappropriate with me in emails," Karen, a hotel assistant manager told me at the start of our call. I had just gotten off the phone with whom I believed was a former scorned lover attempting to get his ex-girlfriend fired from her job by using the hotline to spread lies from an anonymous "concerned citizen." My ears perked up because I just knew Karen's report was about to be good and X-rated. I was eager for her to tell me about what David, who was also an assistant manager, said to her in emails that had gotten her all hot and bothered - I mean upset. "He said good grief it was just a fun way for the team to let their hair down, and not take themselves so seriously." I sat there waiting for Karen to get to the part where David had been inappropriate. "Hello, are you still there?" Karen assumed that the line disconnected because I had yet to respond to what she said. "I'm still here Karen, I didn't want to interrupt you from recalling the other details from the incident, please continue." What she said next really made me wish that the call would disconnect or that the servers went down. Where is Nick Sparrow when you need him? "Well that was it, who responds to anyone saying "good grief", it's unprofessional." Yep, I was definitely talking to Karen. I took a deep breath and exhaled slowly. "So you're offended that David started his email response with good grief? Please pardon me, but I'm struggling to understand how that response could offend you? Karen was going to make it make sense that day. "Are you serious, can I speak to someone else?" Even though I had already heard enough of her, I refused to allow her to torment another innocent unsuspecting coworker. "Unfortunately, ma'am, all other agents are servicing other callers, would you like to give us a call back?" I began a mental countdown because I knew that it was only a matter of time before she said, "I want to speak to a manager!" I knew it was coming. "To be frank ma'am, the established details of your concern do not warrant a manager to intervene to process it." Out of nowhere, Shannon wraps me up in a bear hug from behind and whispers "Thanks" in pure gratitude. I then encouraged Karen to call back at a more opportune time, just in case she was having a change of heart about reporting the issue. "No, I guess I'll get this over with." She was operating in delusion and must have forgotten that she contacted the hotline to complain, and not the other way around, but we continued the call. Once Karen stepped away from her ego, she told me her name had been placed on the list of people who had yet to post a corny joke on the hotel's social media. "I really don't see the point of us making jokes since we are supposed to be professional. All I asked was to have my name removed from the list, and that's the response he chose to give." I'll also have you know that David responded to her email at 7 am, and she reported "the issue" promptly at 5:01 pm, since she had just gotten off at 5 pm, sharp. "Who does he think he is speaking to me that way? I have a Master's degree in Hotel Administration, this hotel begged for me to work here, and this is the respect I get! He owes me an apology. Karen had also reported the issue to Mason, the manager who actually chuckled when she told him her problem, but removed her name from the list. "And by the way, my contract ends tomorrow, but I don't intend to report to work for my official last day." I could imagine that Karen's peers would be happy to hear the news. I was happy for them too! "So are you resigning from the company?" Morphing back into her smug persona, Karen replied, ``Feel free to call it what you want, but I am not coming back!" And just like that, she hung up.

Karen had gotten in her own way. She was so pleased with her educational background that she used it instead of developing a personality and rapport with coworkers. She completely missed an opportunity for her coworkers to respect her as a person, and not just a professional. Anyone from a mile away could see that David's email was an attempt to be lighthearted, non-offensive, and human. Karen refused to view it that way, however. In the time she took to stew in her mess of a wounded ego, she could have asked David how he meant his comments. Honestly, David wasn't even her problem because Karen was playing herself. She blew the situation out of proportion, especially since her name was removed from the list. She was even willing to breach the contract she had established with the company in an effort to massage her hurt feelings. Karen lacked mastery of self and misidentified her opponent, which resulted in self-sabotage. Her approach to addressing the problem, that only existed in her mind, was the equivalent of pushing all the buttons on the controller and expecting to win. So when Karen calls back to say that she didn't get paid according to the contract, I'll be happy to remind her that she had elected to not fulfill it. She finished herself.

Chapter Check

1. Who are the players?

2. What are their powers?

3. How can what they have become of use to me?

4. How do I position myself to win?

Who's Gotcha

There are times, when you will need someone to assist with resolving more grave and serious matters within the workplace such as harassment, discrimination, fraud, and theft to name a few. Yes, employees are stealing more than just pens and markers from the workplace. I took a report where the caller reported a nurse for stealing medication from patients, which is another story for another day. Time and opportunity are all some need to do the deed.

I have taken the calls of employees reporting their managers for not addressing an issue with another employee because of a close friendship. This is also a common occurrence based on numerous reports I have documented about HR's failure to take action in response to recurring issues within the workplace. I understand that the role of HR personnel varies, but what remains constant is their allegiance to the company. Make no mistake about this, the sooner you understand the role of HR, the sooner they can be used as allies. However, there are other resources that can be utilized to get results.

Take Notes

First on this list are detailed notes. Take them. Frequently and often. Your notes can assist mid-level and top-level management with making well informed decisions regarding matters that need to be resolved, and preferably in your favor. Detailed notes have saved me plenty of times while on assignment for different missions. There was one assignment that involved me working at a security company called Locked Down Security Solutions, where a manager had given me a difficult time. This woman, who shall remain nameless, was a micromanager at best, and doubled-minded dictator at her worst. She wanted to undermine every decision I made, which had all been based on the company's policies. I had developed a detailed strategy on how to prevent potential security breaches from occurring, but she quickly dismissed the strategy. "Well, that's not how we'll do it, we're going to do it my way," she said in a high pitched nasally voice. Her voice should have been my first clue that she and I would not mix well. I knew immediately that her luggage was packed and ready for the ego trip she had planned for the next two nights. My projected plan had been considered from every angle, to ensure complete security of the perimeter, while her directions left specific areas open and vulnerable to repeated triggers and potential infiltration, but she wanted her way. Well, that night proved to be very eventful. Those security alarms wailed and yelled like cats in heat all night long. I ran so much that night that my silk press shrank back to Wakanda. While her wig tilted like T.I.'s cap, we functioned very inefficiently, but it was the way she wanted things to be. I could tell she knew she made the wrong decision, but was probably too tired to admit it. I vowed to never work with that woman again after night number two. It wasn't until three months later that I was assigned to work with Ms. Nameless, and my heart dropped down to my feet. I was disappointed, but kept a poker face. I approached the lead security manager, Mr. Chesnutt, who had given me the assignment, and asked to be reassigned. I started having flashbacks of the ringing alarms, and the constant running up and down the perimeter, and then I remembered my beautiful silk press. I could not let it go down like that a third time. "Sir, I am prepared to leave for the evening if you are unable to honor my request," and I meant what I said in the humblest way possible. I promise you this man looked as if he wanted to have me drug tested instead, but he said "Ok Ms. Woodson (my alias at the time), write up an incident report detailing your reasons for refusing the assignment, then report back to me." Mr. Chesnutt's strategy was for me to commit career suicide, by hand delivering my refusal to HR the following morning, because we worked at night. What he did not account for was that I had maintained a detailed record of my notes which provided justification for why I had refused to work with this individual. I gave Mr. Chesnutt a copy of my report to review. He read it and immediately changed his mind about me speaking to HR about the matter. "Ms. Woodson, I, I, I suggest we just have a conversation inst-st-stead." I heard a rumor that Mr. Chestnut stuttered when he was flustered. "Sir, I really don't believe the conversation is necessary because I told her that her actions were counterproductive to my performance of duty already. I'm only seeking for you to grant the privilege of being reassigned." I knew I sounded frigid, and maybe I was, but I was deathly serious about not working with this woman. After much convincing, I agreed to meet with Mr. Chesnutt, and Ms. Nameless. She came in and the smug look on her face slowly disappeared after he read to her, word-for-word the details of my report. My detailed notes included every policy this woman had violated during the two days I worked with her. My notes also disclosed the detail of my plan to safeguard the perimeter, and the decision she made that compromised our surveillance duties. At first, she wanted to deny her actions, then she resorted to deflection before finally acknowledging that she knew my plan was more foolproof, but had disregarded it anyway. Mr. Chesnutt granted my request shortly after our "pow wow." I ended up not having to work with the woman any more after that incident because she and I together were bad for business. Before fully understanding why I refused to work with Ms. Nameless, Mr. Chesnutt's idea was for me to place myself on the chopping block and to sacrifice my career on my own, but my notes had him stopping the guillotine from being dropped on his peer. Mission averted.

"They called me into the office, and they're like, you didn't complete your survival training." Noah Goldfinch, a fellow agent who also worked at LDSS, had management accuse him of being in violation of policy for not attending survival training. Noah had been on vacay during the time the training was facilitated, and no one followed up with him about it when he returned. Noah is probably one of the agency's most methodical and thorough agents; and never takes anyone's word as fact until after he has verified the information himself. "They hand me a paper and tell me to sign it. "You know me, I refused to sign it on the spot. Nothing was making sense though. I went on vacation then boom! You didn't train on how to survive now sign this paper." He animatedly recalled imitating Mr. Warren, the training coordinator. "So, I ask them to please allow me to speak to Chadwick because I am officially rebutting these allegations." Noah's request was granted, and Noah went to work researching the training course and learned that it was still available. It was also during this time that we discovered that we were both agents for the same organization on separate missions. Noah checked emails to see if he had received training notifications before and during his vacay, and he had not. Noah compiled a file of his findings to prepare him for his meeting with Chadwick the director. "He was a hard one to crack, and I could tell he really wanted to substantiate the write up, but I showed him the information I gathered. He didn't have a choice." Noah's write up was thrown out along with everyone else, who had been written up for the same reason.

HR

I know I just low-key blasted HR but hear me out. If you ever think you will have to report a manager for any violation, it will behoove you to obtain a copy of your employment personnel file first. This file will contain any and everything that is relevant to you being an employee. If you have write-ups, check to see when they expire. Also check for your signature on documentation you are unfamiliar with. Review previous and current remarks made from management about your work performance and other details you may be curious about. Clean up what needs to be cleaned up and clarify the unclear, because once you decide to report Kendrick, the manager who insinuated sitting on his lap, may help you get that raise or the promotion you've had your eye on, to HR, things may go from zero to "You're fired" real quick. If you remain ignorant to what is in your employee file, it is subjected to becoming more padded than black market booty shots.

I once spoke to a guy who told me that his manager would have other staff members falsify information in former employees' personnel files to hinder their chances of collecting unemployment benefits after being terminated for reasons outside of misconduct. In some states, misconduct must be proven before a person is denied unemployment due to termination. CHECK. YOUR. FILES.

Your level of employment with a company will at times determine how HR engages with you. HR acted more conservatively toward me as an hourly employee at Luxurious Parking when I sought advice from them on an issue I ended up handling on my own. Word got back to me that Jet was engaged in some conversations that could potentially compromise my integrity. I spoke to Denise, the company's HR representative about the issue. I told her that Jet had made certain comments about me that revealed a gender bias and ultimately projected me in a negative light. I should also mention that for the longest time, I was the only female employed in the branch that I worked. During the conversation, Denise prefaced every statement she made with "If you think," instead of giving me straight answers to my direct questions. The information and advice I received from her became more direct once I became management. Denise was more accessible and transparent with me as a manager when I went to her for advice on how to properly address an employee for performance issues.

Also keep in mind that any formal grievances filed through HR are documented on your employment record, which means you have marked yourself as an individual who has the potential to become disruptive in the workplace. It's funny how that works right? You go to report a problem, and then become the problem for reporting it.

HR carries an obligation to not allow management to become blindsided by allegations that could put the company at risk, so to them it is okay if your privacy is compromised. Your concern or grievance will also be documented on your employment record, which establishes a history of you having issues with management. On the contrary, if management speaks to HR about you, then you will find out as soon as they believe you need to. Let that marinate.

Liz Ryan has pinned numerous articles about her experiences as a person in HR. She recalled noticing that supervisors and managers approached her with more confidence than line staff did. She surmised that management had the understanding of HR being present to advise them on how to manage staff, which all contributes to making shareholders comfortable with their investments into corporations. Ryan also revealed that some of the managers she encountered felt embolden to ask her about the conversations she had with line staff. Ryan was purposeful about being an agent of change within the landscape of her workplace by maintaining confidential conversations with staff members across the board. Hopefully, more HR employees will aspire to be like Liz Ryan, but until that happens, I'll continue to take complaints about those who don't.

Pay it Forward Write a Review

More people have taken to posting the details of their negative work experiences on social media, which include play-by-play details of how they were wronged. This is also an effective means of bringing attention to issues that remain unaddressed because the companies are not in a position to control the narrative of the person who was wronged during the encounter. Releasing formal statements hardly work anymore because the expectations are now for visible improvements to be made. When corporations fail to respond to scandals that involve scorned former employees, their businesses become subject to boycotts, and strikes on top of negative publicity.

Melody, who worked for one of the major automobile brands was being sexually harassed by her boss. She reported the issue to HR who told her she could either transfer to a different team, or subject herself to retaliation from her boss during her performance evaluation. Talk about a lose-lose situation. Melody eventually resigned from the company, but started to blog about her experience. Her blog picked up so much steam that her former employer was forced to take notice and action to address other allegations of misconduct that had occurred within the organization. By sharing her negative one-star experiences, Melody was still able to influence the positive changes that were eventually made to improve her former workplace.

There are also support groups and forums where others who have had similar experiences share advice and resources on how to successfully navigate an issue. Companies such as Blind, Bravely, Loris.ai, and Empower Work are some outside options to explore when the necessary occurs.

Lawyer Up

The language of the law is rich and very layered, which means that if you research, you may find a law that can be applied to your benefit. Certain workplace incidents can crossover into illegal and unlawful territory, and if that happens, it helps for you to know your rights as a person and an employee. Attorneys are great sources for advice and strategy, and if they can argue how your company mishandled you and make them pay for it, then it may be worthwhile. What you say will always carry weight when the right ears are listening.

EEOC

Governmental organizations can be extremely helpful when dealing with matters of discrimination and other injustices. You must strike at the right time. As soon as your suspicions are confirmed, speak to the EEOC at length about the issue. They can also provide guidance on how to further pursue a resolution to the issue as well.

Doris is one of my earliest coaches in the agency, who shared her story of when she had to reach out to the EEOC regarding a matter that pointed in the direction of discrimination. As Doris explained it, she was at the top of her game at You Owe Me Collection Agency, and her sights were set on securing the position of Credit Analyst which would be considered a promotion. Doris met all of the qualifications. She had been a collector for three years; which exceeded the requirement for a candidate to have been in their current role for two years. The company had already started to cross-train Doris on credit analyst duties, so being awarded the position would have been a smooth transition for her. Let's not leave out that Doris had become an unofficial trainer for the newer employees. Doris had more than earned her keep with the company, and now it was time for them to pay up in the form of a promotion. Well, a new kid on the block, Joey decided he wanted to move up the ranks a little faster than scheduled, so he also applied for the position and got it. Joey had barely been with the company for nine months and should not have been allowed to pursue the position. Joey had also been one of Doris's trainees. Doris was livid but remained composed when she asked HR for a copy of the posted vacancy. Once she received her copy, she approached Wyatt, the manager about being overlooked for the promotion. The explanation she received was that Joey had a degree. Doris quickly pointed out there was no education requirement for the position, which meant Joey did not meet any of the other qualifications. Wyatt remained unmoved, so Doris moved on to the EEOC who confirmed that she had been victim to a form of discrimination in the workplace. Doris is an African-American female, where Joey was a Caucasian, so it was a toss-up between it being gender or racial discrimination, I suppose. Wyatt and Joey had more in common, if you catch my drift. The EEOC instructed Doris to report to work as normal, and to not deviate from any routine, so that she could not be accused of neglecting duties and being resentful. Doris followed the EEOC's instructions and then Viola! HR delivered her the good news that she was being promoted.

Doris had to fight twice as hard to receive what was rightfully hers, but she got it.

Stay on The Prowl

Keep your resume polished and updated. You may have to start vetting new job prospects, and you will save time in doing this if you keep your resume current. Networking may also yield new and unique opportunities. If you do not believe that your resume will effectively gain you an interview, then hire a professional to do it for you. More4lessresumes (@more4lesssresumes) has some awesome reviews. I attended a virtual resume writing workshop that the company hosted and got lots of game on how to organize resumes.

RedInk'd (@RedInk'd) is another company that will curate the perfect resume from start to finish. LinkedIn, Fairygodboss, and indeed.com are some other useful resources that can be utilized to get advice, and job leads.

Interview to Find your Soulmate

I learned this tip from XOnecole.com. There was an article that advised readers to treat an interview as if it is a first date. Show up as the best representation of yourself. Not only do you want to give the perfect answers to the hiring panel's questions, but make sure they answer yours correctly too. When you have impressed the interviewer, they will try to do the same in return. An interview is the "getting to know" phase that determines if either party is interested in long-term possibilities. I applied the same principles during the interview of my current assignment. I am introverted by nature and prefer one-on-one and small groups in most cases. I interviewed with a panel of four managers, which felt intimidating. They were all very welcoming people, which allows a candidate to be more relaxed with who they are, smart tactic on their part. They threw out typical interview questions and I answered in an authentic way. But I also had questions of my own. The questions I asked allowed me to determine which individual I had the most in common with when it came to approaching the position I was being "vetted" for. Shannon complimented me on how I flipped the interview session and put them on the spot. Patricia became so comfortable with me that she let a few expletives slip. Anyone walking past the interview room would have thought that we were all friends chopping it up on a lunch break because we were having such a great time. It was no surprise that we felt the same about me joining the team.

"I interview for jobs I don't want to practice my skills," My friend Gerald revealed to me. Gerald enjoyed his job as an accountant, he just never wanted to grow complacent in his abilities to market himself for better opportunities. This would be similar to going on 10 Tinder "practice" dates to ensure that you are comfortable enough to impress the person you are really after, or like married couples having date night to maintain the spark.

I put this strategy to use for a vacancy within the WeCare Reporting Line. I did not get the position, but am now familiar with the company's internal interview process. My gut tells me that M.E. had a hand in me not getting the job.

Chapter Check

1. How detailed are my notes?

2. Have I exhausted all of my options?

3. If so, who should I reach out to next?

The Art of Letting Go

I know I have been heavily advocating for you to take action and matters into your own hands as much as possible, but the truth is that some things will be outside of what you can control. It is a crappy feeling to do everything you can to win and still lose. You start to waver in what you believe, but defeat is not your cue to give up. Defeat simply presents you the opportunity to learn a new fighting style. Enter the art of letting go. Instead of fighting to keep that job that has been trying hard to phase you out anyway, how about building your confidence to know you will be okay regardless? Do you hold on to a faulty charger that can no longer recharge your iPhone battery? No, you will toss that cord in the trash without a second thought. After you have flipped the cord, and angled your phone exactly right, and still do not get a charge? You are done with it because that source of power is frayed, weak, inoperable, no longer serves a purpose for you. Sometimes, the more you struggle, the more it hurts. Let it go. Seek another source, a more powerful, abundant source. I seek God for my peace, sanity, and clarity. He is the one that makes my falling look like flying.

Rashad's Story

Rashad was a former specimen analyst for a laboratory called Fluid Examiners. He called into report that he had been wrongfully terminated. Rashad's character was not as squeaky clean as he would have me to believe it was, but through our conversation, it appeared that who he may have been in the past was being held against him, or maybe even used to set up what turned out to be his fate with the company. "The situation was getting heated, so I walked away to get some air, that's all I did." Rashad said that his arch nemesis, Kate had confronted him about spreading a rumor that she used to put the wrong name on the patients' lab results when the lab received rush orders from medical providers. "We've never liked each other, but I didn't have a reason to sabotage her." Rashad said that Kate stormed into the laboratory while he was in the middle of processing the results of a patient's blood sample, when she started to accuse him of lying on her. "I told Kate, unlike her, I needed to concentrate to make sure the right results were assigned to the right patient, which really teed her off. Her pupils started dilating and she started breathing heavy." Rashad had partially instigated the incident but maintained that he had not been the one to start the rumor, though I could tell he got satisfaction from throwing it up in her face. "Next thing I know, she leaves the room crying and Thomas, the manager comes in chastising me. I think they may have had a lil side deal going on after hours, if you know what I mean." Rashad goes on to tell me that he and Thomas engaged in a yelling match, which was rapidly escalating. "I walked away to put some space between us. When I came back, Big Jack, the security guard was asking for my badge and telling me per management, I could not reenter the building and they would give me a call to tell me when I could; I got fired the next week." After his initial call, I spoke to Rashad approximately 7 times after that because he called daily to see if the company had considered giving him his job back. Rashad told me HR was giving him the runaround and he wanted answers. I realized that Rashad did not actually need an answer regarding the issue, he wanted a different answer because he refused to accept the one he had been given. It was over for him at Fluid Examiners, but he did not want to move on. He did not want to concede to the fact that he no longer worked for the company because he believed he still should have. Rashad was clinging to a past situation instead of moving forward. He already did not have the best reputation with the company (his words), being terminated presented him with the chance to reinvent himself. That's what you are supposed to do after a breakup- show your ex that you got better for your next! Just don't forget to put the old you at the top of your list of exes.

Anna's Story

I am reminded of another story that one of my coworkers, Frank from WeCare Reporting Line, shared with me. He told me a story about a woman named Anna, who had just gotten fired from her job. "She was all over the place with her story. One moment, she was yelling, then crying the next." Frank has a very patient and soothing demeanor, which eventually helped Anna to calm down to report the remainder of her concerns. He took his time and became a listening ear for her. There were things she just needed to get off her chest. Frank and Anna remained on the phone for approximately one hour, but Anna seemed to be refreshed with a burst of energy by the end of the call. She thanked Frank for allowing her to be vulnerable and feel all her emotions as they came and went. Frank told me Anna asked him for the company's address because she still wanted to express her gratitude to him.

Frank brought Anna's gifts in for me to see one day. Anna had made him different origami figures and had written out each letter of his name in her native language. Anna also wrote Frank a letter thanking him for how he had helped her. What stood out most to me was Anna thanking Frank for helping her to choose peace. Anna wrote, "I don't care what happens with the company or the report anymore because I chose peace".

Rashad and Anna were both jilted by how the relationships with their former employers ended, but Anna accepted the reality of fate more sooner than Rashad and became better as a result. Anna released her rage and anger to make room for herself to move on in a positive way. Once she let go, life inspired Anna to create art and share it with Frank. Rashad continued to waste his energy trying to fight a useless cause by calling the center to see if the company had changed their mind. Eventually, they too stopped responding.

Chapter Check

1. What does the next step look like for me?

2. How can I prepare myself to take the next step?

3. Am I fighting the opportunity to evolve?

And Another Thing

The workplace, at times can be a sunken place so use your power to get out. (Couldn't you imagine James Brown saying the last part?) I am now fully purged from today's toxins and feel as light as feather and as free as a bird. I am expecting a call from M.E. to discuss my discoveries from today's operations. I am yet another step closer to entering the evacuation phase, but who knows, I might find myself smack dab in the middle of a real scandal. M.E. mentioned earlier that there is a ring of rogue employees taking over. He did not give me any specifics, but it sounds delicious.! Oh, there's the bird call, gotta go.

Phoenix Files

---

1. Always stay mindful of your triggers. There are times when our minds will make a situation worse than what it may be. If this happens, figure out what was it that set off your internal alarms, but do not stop there. Once you have located the root of your issue, address it within yourself first before taking the next steps to address it with someone else.

2. Say something. Far too often, we believe that words get lost in translation, but who can account for the words left unsaid. Never underestimate the power of your words.

3. After you have checked your triggers, you can speak from a collected place. Be strategic with what you say and how you say it, and always be considerate of your audience.

4. Take accountability for as many factors as you can no matter how difficult it can be. Being accountable for your actions allows you to identify the internal hurdles you must overcome. It is okay to be wrong; and yes, being called to the carpet is uncomfortable, but it will happen a lot less when you take ownership of your shortcomings.

5. It is not always likely for you to find help that you need within the workplace or within your immediate support system in life, but that should not stop you from seeking it. When you cannot find help and assistance from within, then look out.

6. Use the skills that you already have as a foundation to develop more. Grow. Expand and then put it on your resume. Your current employer may be able to determine the length of your employment, but have no say in your life's destiny. You are your own calling card, so always stay ready to answer.

7. Above all, choose peace over everything and never leave home without it.

8. You'll never know how potent your powers are until you learn how to use them.

Phoenix Out

If you are reading this, then I have officially evacuated the building. I would usually leave without a trace, but decided to leave my coworkers with golden keys as parting gifts. The mentality of these people unlocked the door to many limitless possibilities.

I felt like I was in the twilight zone when I first started. Everyone at We Care Reporting Line was eerily nice. I still would not be surprised to find out they were robots with the best human features and characteristics I have ever seen. That is probably why M.E. would not allow me any special spy gear because he knows that I would figure it out. The managers and employees have a uniquely positive rapport with one another. Conflict and tension did not last long around there. I waited patiently for the "other shoe" to drop, but it never did.

If more companies modeled themselves after this one, then We Care Reporting Line would need to find a new business to start.

The comparisons between WeCare Reporting Line versus Who Cares Complaint Line are glaring. The first notable change is personal growth and maturation. I am more aware of myself. The issues that would have triggered alarms in the past, no longer do. You remember what M.E. said about "initiating" mishaps? Let's just say that in the past, my attitude threw certain missions slightly off track. It also helps that We Care Reporting Line prides themselves on their culture. You know how most organizations present themselves as a "We Are the World" place to work, but really "This Is Sparta" once you're hired? Well, We Care Reporting Line is not that. M.E. had already set it up for me to be hired, but I still had to interview for the job, so I respected the process and asserted real effort in making them WANT to hire me. It was a great experience and M.E. was thoroughly impressed with how I interviewed. He managed to have listening devices placed inside the interview room of course. He told me later, "You always keep a trick up your sleeve, you actually convinced them that you wanted this job." I was refreshed by how genuine the interviewers were. They all seemed to enjoy their jobs and actually like each other. I am generally able to quickly assess and detect deception, but I sensed none during the interview, and had yet to do so while continuing the assignment. I have also been maintaining a well updated profile on every single staff member within this company for other investigative purposes that may or may not be revealed later. In one word, this experience has been unique from my end of the phone. I certainly can attest to the reality that mindsets are contagious, and let's just say I called out "sick" a lot at Who Cares Complaint Line. The agency remained patient, but monitored me closely on that assignment out of concern that I would go off the grid. WeCare Reporting Line is far from perfect, but I quickly learned the formula to their success.

I was able to have a brief chat with Shawn and Mario, the co-CEOs for WeCare Reporting line on my way to the breakroom one day. They complimented me on how well I adjusted to the job in a short timeframe. I also won "Employee of the Month," during the third month of being on there. M.E may have warned me not to make a scene at work, but he certainly did not say that I could not be one of the company's top performers. It was during our conversation that I was able to dig deeper into the psyches of these masterminds. "Well, in the beginning, we knew that we wanted to make a difference, we just didn't know how," said Mario; the most energetic of the pair. "We've had a ton of business ideas, but none of them seemed to stick, so we kept with it," I expected Shawn the grounded one to have this perspective. Their energies seemed to complement each other just like everyone else's. "We realized the only true way to make a difference was to find a problem to solve." They explained how the research for developing their business led them down a unique path. "After realizing there were so many employees who genuinely dislike their jobs, our first strategy was to figure out why." Mario was getting charged up again. "But then we realized there were a million reasons for a person to not like their job, but then Shawn had an idea. Mario was eager for Shawn to tell the rest of the story about their journey to success. "Well, we narrowed the research down to why the people who worked in the same industry as us disliked their jobs, and started there. We scoured the job board reviews of our competitors and read in detail about why their employees were dissatisfied and had even quit." The more they learned about the challenges their competitors were unable to conquer, the more strategic they became. "What we deduced was that just because the employees of our competitors hated their jobs, it did not mean that they were not good at what they did." Mario and Shawn were determined to hire good people, character being the most important, but experience being a strong second. "Our competitors had already trained their staff; which meant they were familiar with reporting processes and dealing with disgruntled people, so we recruited them away from the company and invited them to work with us." Mario and Shawn believed that in order for them to have a thriving successful company, they needed good people who enjoyed the work that they did. "We joked a lot about being rehab for disgruntled call center workers, but the reality is that we are. We believed that our employees were great assets from the start, and we treated them as such." "We have a 10 out of 10 success rate for converting skeptics into believers simply because we are the embodiment of our standards, but not in a stuffy way. We pride ourselves in taking a human approach to human beings. There's really no other way to do it, unless you hire robots, but then you have a brain with no heart." That explained so much about what I had witnessed among Mario, Jared, and Oliver on my first day. Jared was previously the victim of a hostile work environment, and while he was an extremely talented employee; he was cutthroat in his approach to tackling the job. Instead of writing him off as a "lost cause," the team banded together to support Jared in shifting his mindset. Where he once operated in survival mode, Jared now functioned to thrive. "This is a safe place for success," Mario said with a wink. WeCare Reporting Line are industry leaders because two people were determined to find a problem and solve it.

My time at WeCare Reporting made it easier and clearer to understand how some go wrong with just allowing a complaint to remain a complaint instead of allowing it to evolve into a growth opportunity.

As much as I learned to enjoy the company itself, I am over the moon that I will not have to retire there. How I despised the screeching sounds of a complaint! To be fair, I did speak to several individuals who needed help and wanted to be heard; while there were others who only wanted to "vent" in order to recycle their negative energy. I was assigned the duty of infiltrating the WeCare Reporting Line to understand their unique approach to extracting information from the callers to report back to their employers, and it was just as Mario and Shawn said, they take a human approach to human beings. My mission within that duty was to get you to elevate your mindset and the value you place in your abilities to advocate for yourself, not just at work, but in life as well. The moment that you believe you win, then you will, and the same applies to losing.

Complaining is a trait of the lazy person. Sure, procedures must be followed at work, but choosing to never find the strength lying dormant within you is lazy, and you will never be fulfilled in your purpose or in life because you expect for another human being to do that for you. A problem is only as big as you allow it to be, but as soon as you start chipping away at the predicament, you become large enough to conquer it. Accept my challenge to rise to the occasion. I guarantee you the view is much better from up here. Oh yeah and my "farewell" attire was one for the books. Alexa, play *Six Inch Heels* by Beyonce.

P.W. On to the Next

"P. W.

Great work on your last mission. I knew I picked the right person for your job. The information that you were able to obtain for the agency has been invaluable. While I know you were looking forward to soaking up sun rays at a private beach, I am afraid that you will have to put your plans on hold just for a little longer. Remember I mentioned a league of rogue employees laying siege to their workplace? Well, it is worse than what we expected, and deeper than what we initially thought. This mission will call for you to frequently adapt and change to your environment, which should not be an issue because you have a flair for the dramatic. You will also have more fashion choices that Makeba will personally be responsible for. You will be in good company. Nick Sparrow is in the process finalizing the details of the mission as we speak. You will have special equipment to use for completing your tasks. Expect another message from me by midnight. You will head out in two days."

-M. E

"Now that's what I'm talking about! Action and drama! It's about to be a movie. I get to infiltrate a ring of corrupt employees and get up in their business. Yes, sign me up. Twice. I'll hold my breath on the fashions this time, the man said I would have more fashion choices; not better, but I know Makeba will keep a lil' something in the wings for me. I cannot wait to blow the roof off of whatever this scandal is. I will fill you in at midnight, so be ready!

Acknowledgement Page

W hat a journey this has been! I have been full of stories for a very long time, and am so excited that I was finally able to clear some head space to write a book. I thank God firstly because all things are possible with him, and take crazy long to figure out without him. My parents, Dorothy and Robert, I am rich in love because of you. My brother Robert Jr., your determination is inspiring and contagious. Please continue to infect the masses. To my brother Alton, your kindness is your superpower. Kim, you are a rockstar sister-in-law. I admire all the "heart work" you put into making your dreams come true. To my nephews, Oliver and Alton Jr., the world is yours and that is a statement of fact. To my friends however we met, whenever we met, I am forever grateful that our paths crossed. Aunties Madeline and Belinda, I had to acknowledge you because you've been reality checks and sounding boards for me. I would also have to reprint this book if your names were not written in plain text. Auntie Delores, I am always thankful for your thoughtfulness. I would also like to express delayed gratitude to my trials and tribulations because without them there would be no stories to tell or character to develop.